All the drawings that everyone is looking at have been kept in a box that Grandpa Paul stored away in the bottom of an old trunk. When Grandpa Paul was a young man, he was a great balloon pilot. Now, as he looks at the old drawings, he remembers his past adventures.

Anybody who has ever ridden in a balloon will never forget the experience. And someone who has never tried it cannot resist the temptation to take a balloon trip. Grandpa Paul says that making a balloon is not so very difficult. All he needs is a large piece of cloth and

lots of enthusiasm. The Five Friends find it hard to imagine that a balloon made from this huge sheet could possibly lift and carry them to the other side of the world. Only Kip and Grandpa Paul really know the secret of big balloons.

Anchored with a rope, the balloon is ready and waiting to fly. Grandpa Paul adds the finishing touches to the hull while Monica, Tony, and Alex prepare everything they will need for the trip. Kip watches them and

thinks that they all have gone crazy. He thinks it's fine if they want to make a balloon, but to get in it and go for a ride is a very different matter.

Finally, the flight begins. The balloon is full of hot air and lifts up into the sky. From a bird's eye view, the Five Friends discover a new world. All the animals in the woods come to wish the bold travelers good luck.

When you ride in a balloon you are never quite sure where you will go, but today, all the winds are favorable for the flight.

From high above the ground the world looks very small to the Five Friends. This is what they see below: toy countries, cardboard villages, dolls' houses, and tiny doll-sized people waving good-bye. A child's kite passes next to them.

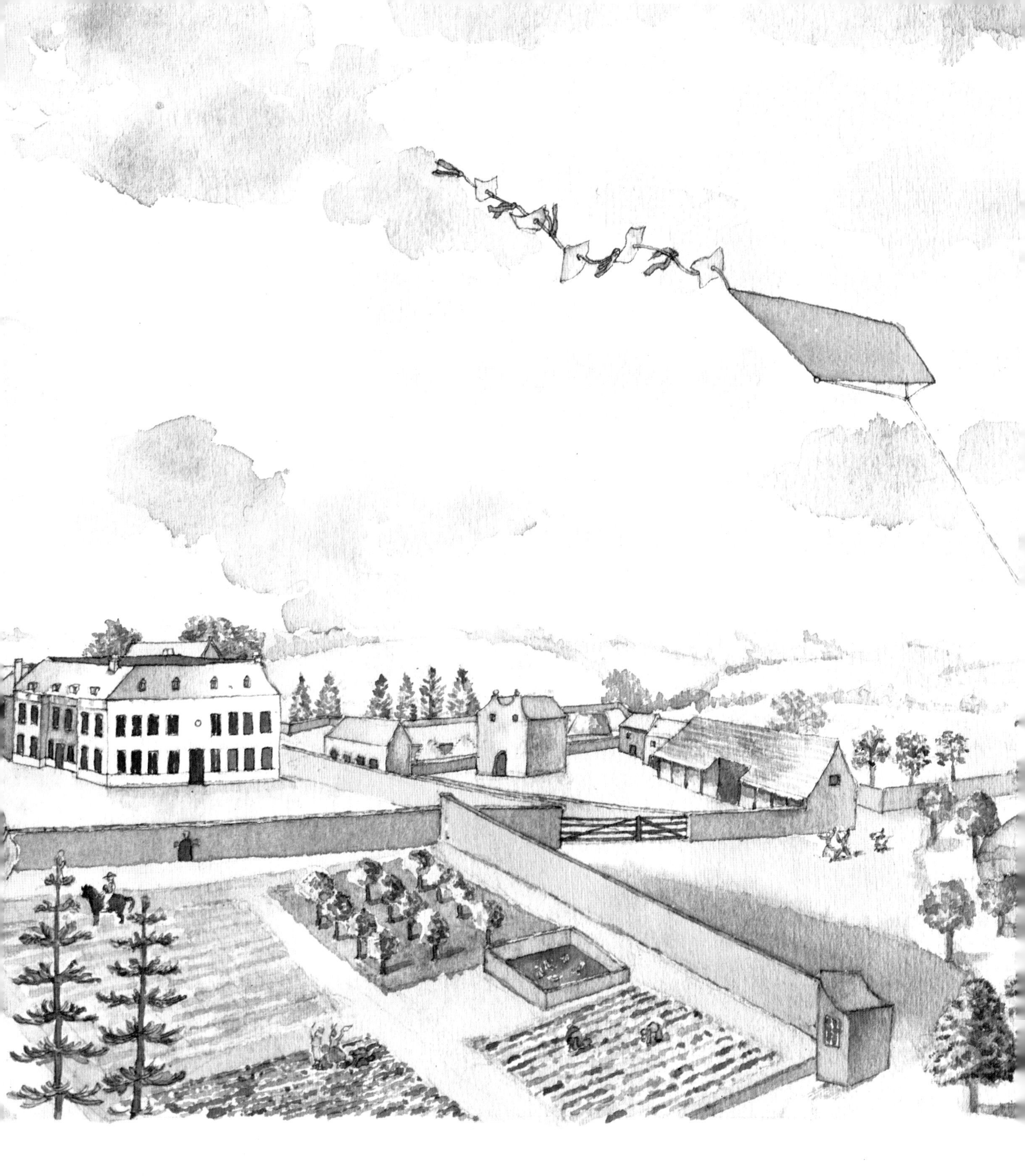

Alex sends down paper airplanes with drawings and messages for his friends who are watching from the ground. They all wish that they, too, were up there in the balloon.

The wind blows the balloon toward the sea. The ships look like nutshells gliding gently over a huge blue carpet. Grandpa Paul consults a map. "Where will this sea wind take us?" the Friends ask him. Only the birds

really know the ways of the winds. Susan looks over toward the horizon and thinks that, if nothing changes, they will end up in China!

Now the balloon passes over a beautiful city filled with palaces, squares, markets, and houses. Watch out! They are heading toward the spire of a church. The balloon must change course or it will crash against it and explode.

Meanwhile, the rooster on the weathervane is amazed by the sight. Suddenly, a wild duck gets tangled in the ropes. Tony and Grandpa Paul free it. The adventurers wonder what the people in the town below think as they watch them pass overhead.

Flying further, they see the mountains again. The silent balloon rocks gently. Not even the shepherd sleeping below notices as they pass. The wildcat sees the balloon, and all the other animals wonder what odd kind

of bird is flying through the sky. In order to see the eagles better, the Five Friends and Grandpa Paul must send the balloon even higher.

Neither the Five Friends nor Grandpa Paul have been watching where they are going. Suddenly, they are surrounded by many other balloons of different sizes and colors. They have drifted into a big race! There is also

an acrobat who has invented strange wings and glides among the balloons. “Wouldn’t it be funny if he were able to fly faster than our balloon?” says Monica.

The Five Friends land in their balloon. This is the end of the trip. It seemed so short! They would like to go for another ride but Grandpa Paul says, "That's enough for today. It has been a wonderful trip." The rest of

the balloons that have been in the race arrive slowly. Meanwhile, a woman from the town looks at them with wonder.

The judges of the race decide to give the Five Friends and Grandpa Paul a special prize for their ride. Everybody is very happy. "We must tell everyone at home," says Susan. "We could make a bigger balloon and fly across the whole world!" says Alex. "It's good to have a dream," says Grandpa Paul.
"Maybe one day we will." "Meanwhile, we can watch for other balloons in the sky," says Tony. "It will be a nice way for us to remember our great adventure."